The Magic School Bus
in the Time
of the Dinosaurs

TEACHERS' MAILBOXES

MR. B | COPELAND | DARVIN

STOTTS | EISENSTADT | FRIZZLE

RATTINER | ROBERTS | SELTZER

FRIZZLE
SCHOOL
USA

The Magic School Bus
in the Time of the Dinosaurs

By Joanna Cole

Illustrated by Bruce Degen

SCHOLASTIC INC.

New York Toronto London Auckland Sydney

The author and illustrator wish to thank
Mark A. Norell, Associate Curator of Vertebrate Paleontology,
the American Museum of Natural History, for his assistance in preparing this book.

For their helpful advice and consultation, thanks also to Armand Morgan,
Public Education Department, Yale-Peabody Museum of Natural History, New Haven, Connecticut;
Professor Leo J. Hickey, Curator of Paleobotany, Yale-Peabody Museum of Natural History;
Dave Varricchio, expert of Tyrannosaurus Rex, Museum of the Rockies, Bozeman, Montana.

ISBN 0-590-44689-4

12 11 10 9 8 7 6   8   6 7 8 9/9 0/0

Printed in the U.S.A.

The illustrator used pen and ink, watercolor, color pencil,
and gouache for the paintings in this book.

To Armand Morgan,
our personal guide to the time of the dinosaurs
J.C. & B.D.

It was Visitors Day at our school.
Parents, relatives, and friends
were coming that afternoon to see our work.
In Ms. Frizzle's class, we were making
the whole room into Dinosaur Land!

Suddenly, Ms. Frizzle said,
"Please pay attention, children.
I have wonderful news!"

I WONDER WHAT THE GOOD NEWS IS.

MAYBE IT'S LUNCHTIME ALREADY.

MAYBE WE DON'T HAVE TO LEARN ALL THESE DINOSAUR NAMES.

A WORD FROM DOROTHY ANN

Prehistoric means anything that happened before people started writing history.

COELOPHYSIS

DIPLODOCUS

TYRANNOSAURUS REX

APATOSAURUS

ALLOSAURUS

DINOSAURS WERE REPTILES
by Carlos

Dinosaurs were a group of special prehistoric reptiles. Reptiles are animals that:
- have backbones
- have scaly skin
- lay eggs
- are cold-blooded

REPTILES OF TODAY

SNAKES

CROCODILES

TURTLES

LIZARDS

RELATED TO A DINOSAUR AND PROUD OF IT!

DINOSAURS WERE SPECIAL

Dinosaurs had straight legs. They could walk or run fast.

Today's reptiles have sprawled-out legs.

"Our class has been invited to a dinosaur dig," explained the Friz.
"We'll be leaving right away."
As we went out, one kid grabbed the video camera.
Others took along model dinosaurs for good luck.
When you have the wackiest teacher in school,
you need all the luck you can get!

WE'RE LEAVING NOW?

I GUESS MS. FRIZZLE FORGOT ABOUT VISITORS DAY.

SHE NEVER FORGOT ANYTHING BEFORE.

Dear
Come and see the dinosaur bones we're digging up. Bring the whole class. Yours, Jeff

Ms. V. Frizzle
SCHOOL
U.S.A.

We couldn't believe we had to get on that rickety old school bus again. Kids held their lucky dinosaurs tight, and hoped for the best.

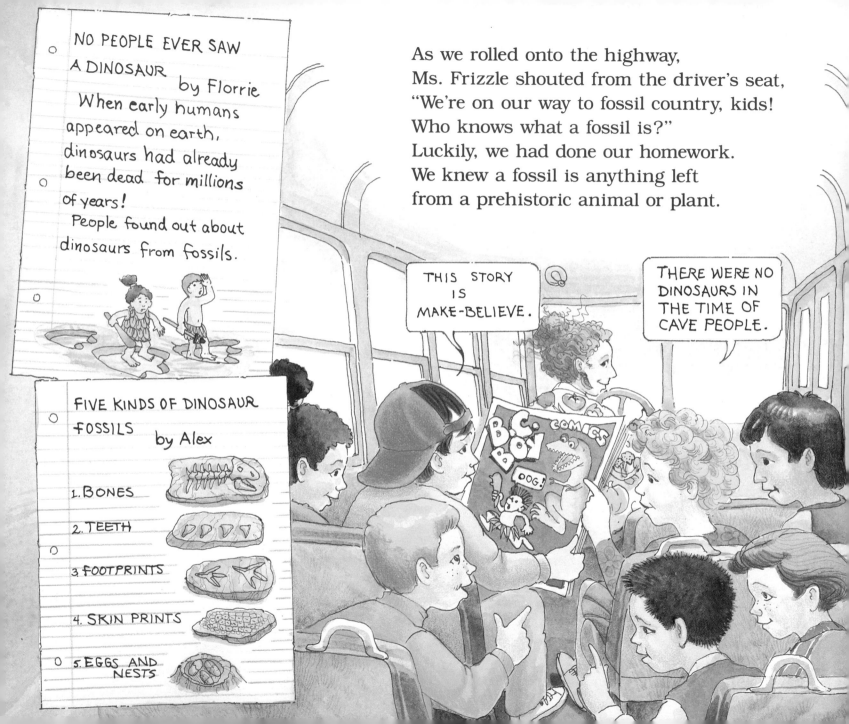

NO PEOPLE EVER SAW
A DINOSAUR   by Florrie
When early humans
appeared on earth,
dinosaurs had already
been dead for millions
of years!
People found out about
dinosaurs from fossils.

FIVE KINDS OF DINOSAUR
FOSSILS   by Alex

1. BONES

2. TEETH

3. FOOTPRINTS

4. SKIN PRINTS

5. EGGS AND NESTS

As we rolled onto the highway,
Ms. Frizzle shouted from the driver's seat,
"We're on our way to fossil country, kids!
Who knows what a fossil is?"
Luckily, we had done our homework.
We knew a fossil is anything left
from a prehistoric animal or plant.

THIS STORY IS MAKE-BELIEVE.

THERE WERE NO DINOSAURS IN THE TIME OF CAVE PEOPLE.

After we had been driving for a long time, we came to a desert where people were working. Ms. Frizzle said this was the dinosaur dig. The people were paleontologists — scientists who study prehistoric life.

We saw a gleam in Ms. Frizzle's eye.
"Want to look for some *Maiasaura* nests,
kids?" she shouted.
She rushed us onto the bus
and drove off.

We hadn't gone far when Ms. Frizzle
stopped the bus.
She turned a dial on the dashboard,
and the bus began to change.
It looked like a giant alarm clock.
Ms. Frizzle said it was a time machine!

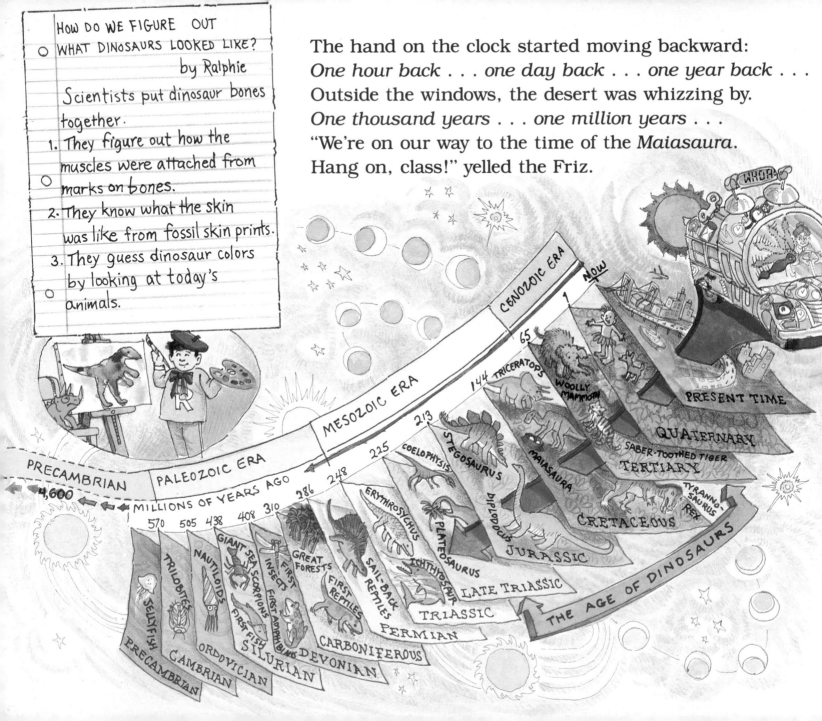

The hand on the clock started moving backward:
One hour back . . . one day back . . . one year back . . .
Outside the windows, the desert was whizzing by.
One thousand years . . . one million years . . .
"We're on our way to the time of the *Maiasaura*.
Hang on, class!" yelled the Friz.

WHOA!

NOW

PRESENT TIME

CENOZOIC ERA

1 WOOLLY MAMMOTH

65 TRICERATOPS

SABER-TOOTHED TIGER

QUATERNARY

TERTIARY

144 MESOZOIC ERA

MAIASAURA

TYRANNOSAURUS REX

213 STEGOSAURUS

DIPLODOCUS

CRETACEOUS

225 COELOPHYSIS

ICHTHYOSAUR

PLATEOSAURUS

JURASSIC

248 ERYTHROSUCHUS

SAIL-BACK REPTILES

LATE TRIASSIC

286 FIRST REPTILES

TRIASSIC

310 GREAT FORESTS

PERMIAN

PALEOZOIC ERA

408 FIRST INSECTS FIRST AMPHIBIAN

CARBONIFEROUS

438 GIANT SEA SCORPIONS FIRST FISH

DEVONIAN

PRECAMBRIAN

4,600

MILLIONS OF YEARS AGO

570 505 NAUTILOIDS

SILURIAN

JELLYFISH

TRILOBITES

ORDOVICIAN

CAMBRIAN

PRECAMBRIAN

THE AGE OF DINOSAURS

Ring! Ring! The alarm went off.
We heard Ms. Frizzle say, "Ooops!
We had a little machine trouble.
We went back too far in time,
but it's nothing to worry about."
Nothing to worry about!
We missed the time of the *Maiasaura*
by millions of years!

WHAT WAS THE EARTH LIKE THEN?

PANGAEA

One giant continent called PANGAEA

- Rainy Jungles
- Many deserts
- Warm temperatures
- No winter anywhere!

CLASS, WE'RE IN THE LATE TRIASSIC PERIOD-- THE TIME OF THE EARLY DINOSAURS!

YOU MEAN WE'RE IN THE SAME PLACE BUT IN ANOTHER TIME?

YOU MEAN THIS IS WHAT THAT DESERT LOOKED LIKE 220 MILLION YEARS AGO?

WOW! IT'S A JUNGLE OUT THERE!

DINODONTOSAURUS

COELOPHYSIS

WHERE WE ARE IN TIME

PRESENT TIME

CENOZOIC ERA 65 MILLION YEARS AGO

CRETACEOUS 144 MILLION YEARS AGO

JURASSIC 213 MILLION YEARS AGO

LATE TRIASSIC 225 MILLION YEARS AGO

FOSSIL TEETH TELL WHAT DINOSAURS ATE
by Phoebe

Sharp, pointy teeth came from meat-eaters.

TYRANNOSAURUS REX
ALLOSAURUS
TROODON

BRUSHING KEEPS YOUR TEETH IN SHAPE WHATEVER SHAPE THEY ARE

Odd-shaped teeth came from plant-eaters.

CAMARASAURUS
PLATEOSAURUS
STEGOSAURUS

The Friz pointed to some dinosaurs that were hunting on the banks of a river. "Their name is *Coelophysis*," she said. "These early dinosaurs were small and light. The giant dinosaurs did not develop until later."

COELOPHYSIS HAVE EXCELLENT TEETH FOR EATING MEAT. THEIR TEETH HAVE "SAW" EDGES LIKE STEAK KNIVES.

TRY NOT TO LOOK LIKE A STEAK!

PREY:
DRAGONFLY
LIZARD
MAMMALS
AMPHIBIAN

Suddenly, a large reptile rose out of the water and opened its huge mouth.
"That is not a dinosaur," Ms. Frizzle said.
"It's a phytosaur — a crocodile-like reptile."
The phytosaur caught a little dinosaur and pulled it underwater.
We wanted to get back on the bus, pronto!
But Ms. Frizzle said we had to learn about Triassic plant life.

ARE MEAT-EATERS MEAN?
by Arnold
No. Predators are part of nature. Hunting is the only way they can get their food.

SOME WORDS FROM DOROTHY ANN
A _predator_ is a hunting animal.
Prey are the animals a predator hunts.

AETOSAUR

PHYTOSAUR

I'M A PREDATOR.

I'M PREY.

We were examining some ferns
when Ms. Frizzle shouted,
"Look at those terrific prosauropods!
They were the first dinosaurs to eat plants!"

CONIFER

PLATEOSAUR

A sudden downpour caught us by surprise.
But the dinosaurs went right on eating.
We ran for the bus, and Frizzle called,
"Get ready to go *forward* in time, kids!"

IN A TROPICAL FOREST,
RAINS ARE FREQUENT
AND HEAVY, ARNOLD.

NOW SHE
TELLS ME!

JEFF WILL
LOVE THIS
VIDEO.

THE FIRST MAMMALS
LIVED WITH DINOSAURS
by Rachel

The first true mammals
lived in the Late Triassic.
They were furry rat-like
animals.

WHAT ARE MAMMALS?
by Wanda
Mammals are animals that:
- have backbones
- have hair or fur
- are warm-blooded

— feed their babies with
mothers' milk

The last things we saw before we took off
were some small, furry animals.
Ms. Frizzle said they were the first mammals.
The hand on the clock moved ahead,
and the Triassic rain forest whizzed out of sight.

WHEN WILL WE SEE
MAIASAURA EGGS?

MAIASAURA LIVED 160 MILLION
YEARS FROM NOW. LET'S SEE
IF WE CAN FIND THEM.

NOW

THEN

LATER

EARLY MAMMALS

WE KNOW DINOSAURS LAID EGGS
by Amanda Jane

Fossil dinosaur eggs have been found. Inside some, there are tiny skeletons of babies.

HOW BIG WERE DINOSAUR EGGS?
by Molly

The largest dinosaur egg we have found was about the size of a football!

Under a pile of leaves, we found some dinosaur eggs just about to hatch!
Nearby some stegosaurs — plated dinosaurs — were eating plants.
One of the stegosaurs had a hurt leg.

ARE THEY THE MAIASAURA EGGS?

NO, KEESHA. MAIASAURA DID NOT LIVE IN THE JURASSIC PERIOD.

THEY CAME LATER. MUCH LATER.

Suddenly an *Allosaurus* approached
the wounded *Stegosaurus*.
Stegosaurus's spiked tail lashed out.
It missed *Allosaurus* by an inch!
What would happen next?
We held our breath.

serrated edge

ALLOSAURUS
TOOTH
(actual size)

IT'S HARD TO BE A HUNTER
by Alex
Being a predator is
dangerous. Predators
can get hurt or killed
by their prey. This is why
meat-eaters often attack
prey that is weak, sick,
or young.

Allosaurus darted close and took a big bite.
Then it moved back and waited.
Stegosaurus got weaker and weaker.
It had become food for *Allosaurus*.

ALL DINOSAURS WERE <u>LAND</u> ANIMALS
by Gregory

No dinosaurs lived in the sea. During the Cretaceous, dinosaurs lived in places that were not covered by water.

WE WON'T SEE ANY DINOSAURS HERE.

Ring! Ring! The alarm went off again.
We looked out — and then we freaked out!
Once again, we had stopped too soon.
"Here we are in the Late Cretaceous Period,"
announced Ms. Frizzle.
"At this time there was a sea
right in the middle of our continent."

WE'RE IN THE SAME PLACE 25 MILLION YEARS LATER.

HOW TIME FLIES.

THAT'S NOT ALL THAT FLIES.

PTERANODON

PRESENT TIME

CENOZOIC ERA
65 MILLION YEARS AGO

CRETACEOUS
144 MILLION YEARS AGO

JURASSIC
213 MILLION YEARS AGO

LATE TRIASSIC
225 MILLION YEARS AGO

WHERE WE ARE IN TIME

Out the windows, enormous sea reptiles swam by.
Overhead, flying reptiles glided past,
dipping their beaks in the water to catch fish.
We were getting a little wet,
so the Friz set the clock ahead again.

I'M HOMESICK.

I'M SEASICK.

AT MY OLD SCHOOL THE BUS DIDN'T LEAK.

CAN'T WE FIND A DRIER TIME, MS. FRIZZLE?

ELASMOSAURUS

ARCHELON

ICHTHYOSAUR

SEA REPTILES AND FLYING REPTILES: WERE THEY DINOSAURS?
by Tim

No, they were relatives of dinosaurs.

HI, COUSIN!

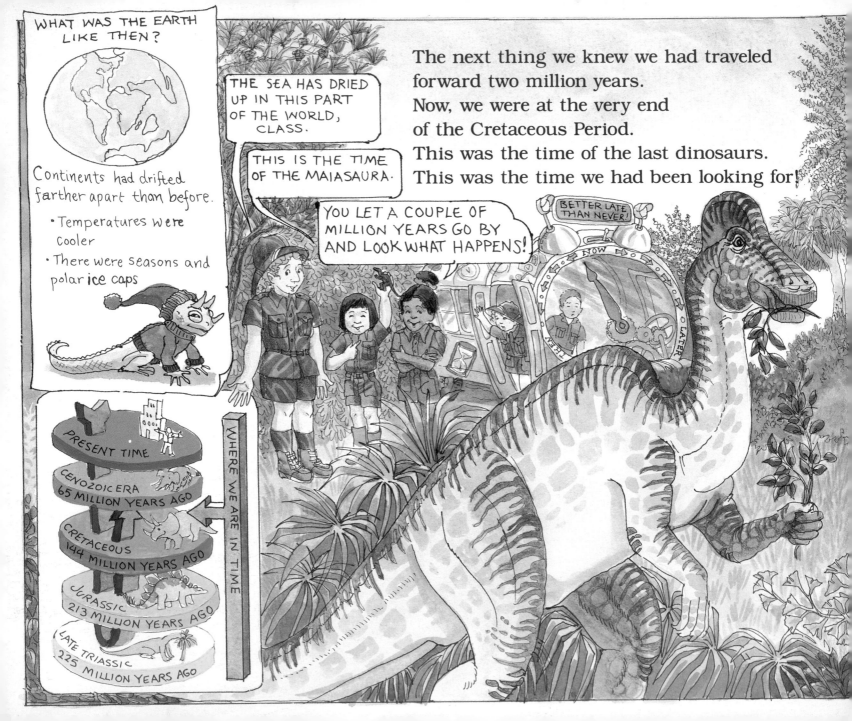

As soon as we got off the bus,
we saw that the Cretaceous world was different.
The weather was cooler.
There were colorful flowers and fruits everywhere.
And there were lots of new plant-eating dinosaurs.
"These plant-eaters could chew better than
any other dinosaurs," said Ms. Frizzle.
"They had terrific teeth for grinding,
and they had *cheeks*!"

CHEEKS KEEP FOOD
FROM FALLING OUT
SO PLANT-EATERS
DO NOT LOSE FOOD
THEY HAVE
ALREADY CHEWED.

GEE, I DIDN'T
KNOW CHEEKS
WERE SO
IMPORTANT.

NEW PLANT-EATERS OF THE
CRETACEOUS PERIOD
by Ms. Frizzle

DUCKBILLS
Had hundreds of
teeth in horny
beaks.

DOMEHEADS
Had thick skulls.
May have butted
heads like rams.

ARMORED
Had armor.
Had few teeth.

HORNED
Had neck frill
and horns. Had
slicing teeth.

DINOSAURS WERE SPECIAL
Some dinosaurs chewed their
food. All of today's reptiles
swallow it whole.

DUCKBILL TEETH
Duckbills had
hundreds of
rows of teeth.

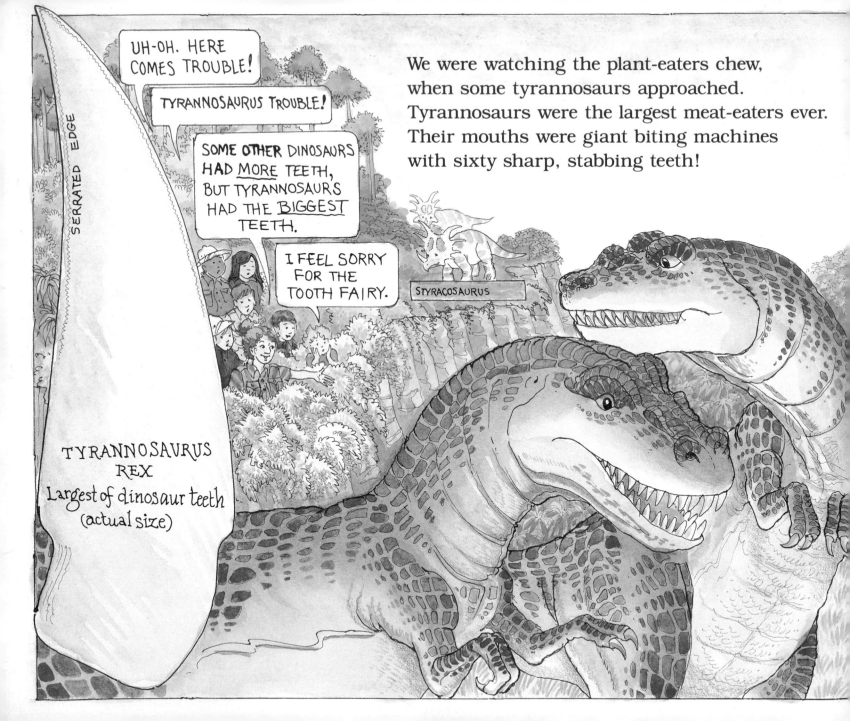

We were watching the plant-eaters chew, when some tyrannosaurs approached. Tyrannosaurs were the largest meat-eaters ever. Their mouths were giant biting machines with sixty sharp, stabbing teeth!

The tyrannosaurs were scary enough.
Then a pack of *Troodon* showed up, too!
They were small, but there were a lot of them!
They began circling the bus to see what it was.
We sized up the situation and ran.

ALL MEAT-EATING DINOSAURS WERE TWO-LEGGED
by Phoebe
Plant-eaters came in all different shapes.

Hadrosaurus Stegosaurus Apatosaurus

But all meat-eaters were built on the same pattern.

Allosaurus Coelophysis Tyrannosaurus Rex

Troodon Tooth (actual size)

I HOPE YOU ARE OBSERVING THE TROODON, CLASS. NOTICE THE SLASHING CLAW ON EACH BACK FOOT.

WE'D LIKE TO OBSERVE THEM, MS. FRIZZLE, BUT...

WE HAVE TO LEAVE... RIGHT AWAY.

IN A HURRY...

THIS INSTANT...

IN OTHER WORDS... NOW!

DINOSAURS WERE SPECIAL
Some dinosaurs may have hunted in packs!
None of today's reptiles do.

TROODON

WHY DO WE THINK MAIASAURA BABIES GREW UP IN NESTS?

by Wanda

When scientists found the first Maiasaura nests, they saw:

• <u>Crushed eggshells</u>, showing that babies might have stayed in nests and stepped on shells.

• <u>Skeletons of different sizes</u>, showing that babies might have grown bigger in nests.

• <u>Worn down baby teeth</u>, showing that babies might have eaten food brought by parents.

We weren't the only ones
who had found the *Maiasaura*.
The *Troodon* had followed us.
They invaded the nesting ground.
The *Maiasaura* parents defended their young.
All at once, a sandstorm blew up.
In minutes, a thick layer of sand
covered the dinosaurs.

THESE DINOSAURS
WILL ALL BE
BURIED.

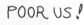

POOR DINOSAURS!

POOR US!

Everything happened so fast.
There was no way we could help
the dinosaurs.
Maybe they would become fossils.

OH, NO!
I DROPPED
MY MODEL
MAIASAURA!

HURRY UP
AND RUN!

Back in the bus, Ms. Frizzle drove
forward in time.
We thought we were going home,
but, on the way,
the bus screeched to a stop.

STRUTHIOMIMUS

PRESENT TIME

CENOZOIC ERA
65 MILLION YEARS AGO

CRETACEOUS
144 MILLION YEARS AGO

JURASSIC
213 MILLION YEARS AGO

LATE TRIASSIC
225 MILLION YEARS AGO

WHERE WE ARE IN TIME

"We are in the very last minutes of the Cretaceous Period," said Ms. Frizzle. A bright light was shining in the sky. "Notice that asteroid," said the Friz. "It's a huge rock from outer space. Soon it will hit the earth."

THE ASTEROID WILL CAUSE AN ENORMOUS EXPLOSION... BLACK SOOT WILL FILL THE AIR AND BLOCK OUT THE SUN... PLANTS WON'T GROW, AND MILLIONS OF LIVING THINGS WILL BECOME EXTINCT — INCLUDING THE DINOSAURS.

MS. FRIZZLE, COULD WE LEAVE BEFORE THE ASTEROID HITS?

LAMBEOSAURUS

The Friz pushed the forward button, and we started again.

WE'RE ONLY 65 MILLION YEARS FROM HOME, CLASS.

STEP ON IT, PLEASE...

When the alarm rang, we were back in our own time.
The paleontologists were worried about us,
and came looking for us.
We gave them a tip on a fossil site.
Then we waved good-bye and drove back to school.

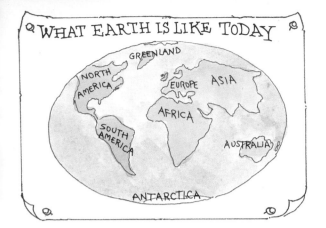

In the classroom, we made a chart
of our trip to the dinosaurs.
Just as we were finishing it,
people started coming in for Visitors Day.

The visitors admired everything.
They had never seen such fabulous projects,
such wonderful books, or such an incredible video.
And, of course, they had never met a teacher
quite like Ms. Frizzle!